Woody

The Kentucky Wiener

Welcomes a Dad

by

Leigh Anne Florence

Illustrations by James Asher

This book is dedicated
in honor of my father and mother-in-law,
B.W. and Gladys Florence
and their 62+ years of marrage.

Thank you for being a strong foundation
and a shining example to so many people
and thank you for providing us all
with a place to call home.

Special Thanks from Leigh Anne

First, as always, to my husband Ron. I cannot begin to tell you how thankful I am for you. Thank you for sacrificing so much to make this dream – our dream - become reality. You are without a doubt the best bus driver, prop man, puppy daddy, manager, and husband a girl could ask for. Being your wife is the greatest honor in the world. I love you forever. Hugs and Kisses!

To all of my friends and family for their amazing support. I wish I could list every single one of you by name. Fortunately, for me, the list is way too long. There are so many of you who have made this project a success. You know who you are and you know the special place you hold in my heart.

To my fellow Kentuckians who welcomed us into their lives with book I, *The Adoption.* Meeting each of you has been such a pleasure. Thank you for allowing us to continue the journey of Woody with this second book. We look forward to many years of sharing Woody's story.

And finally, to my sweet, sweet puppies, Chloe and Woody. Life is so much sweeter sharing every day with you. Thank you for the joy and smiles you bring me every single day. I love being your mommy! You could never know how much I love the two of you!

In TINYTOWN, Kentucky
Is a family of three,
If you look inside their home
Love and happiness you'll see.

1

2

Woody is a wiener dog,
Chloe one as well.
They live with their mommy
And they think she's really swell.

They love how Mommy cares for them.
They think it's really great.
She plays ball with them
and bathes them
And puts goodies on their plate.

4

5

6

They think their life is perfect.
They are happy as can be.
They are oh so very thankful
For their tiny family tree.

"Please come here dear puppies,
Before you take your nap.
I have something to tell you.
Please sit upon my lap."

9

"What is it Mommy?" asked Woody

"Have I been a bad boy?

I ate all my dinner

And I picked up all my toys."

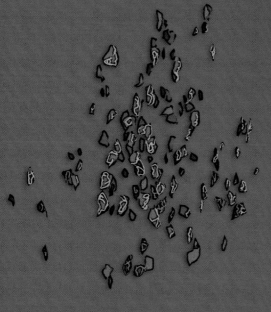

"No, it was me," said Chloe
"I'm the guilty soul.
I wasn't very careful
And I spilled my dinner bowl."

"Oh you little puppies.
Please don't worry or fret.
I just want to talk to you.
I am not upset.

14

What I have to tell you
I think will make you glad.
Mommy's getting married.
You now will have a dad!"

15

"A dad, a dad?" asked Woody
"I can't believe it's true!
Of course I'm happy, Mommy.
Is he a wiener dog too?"

"You're so funny, Woody!
Don't you understand?
Mom's not marrying a puppy
She is marrying a man!"

Woody scratched his little head
Before finally looking up.
"I guess a man's okay.
But I wish he were a pup."

19

"What's the matter, Chloe?
You look a little sad.
Aren't you glad Mom's marrying
And we will have a dad?"

20

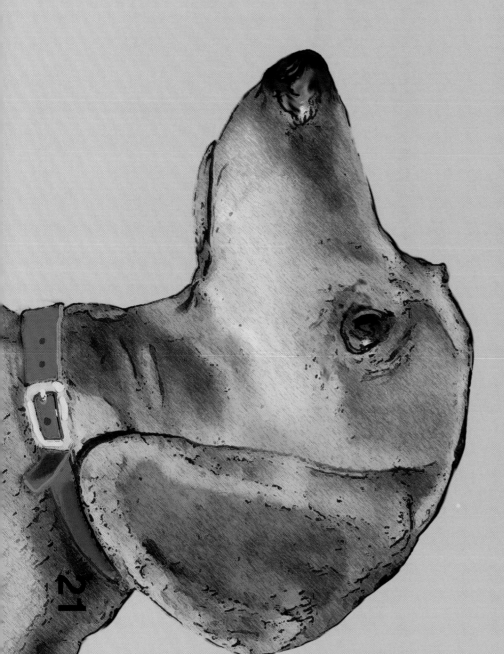

"I am sorry Woody,
if I look a little blue.
What if he loves Mommy
But doesn't love us too?"

21

"Oh my precious Chloe"
Mommy said with tenderness,
"Of course your dad will love you.
He will think you're both the best.

22

23

I know it may be scary
But believe me when I say,
'He will love you very much
and be your dad in every way.'

So please be happy puppies—
No need for being blue.

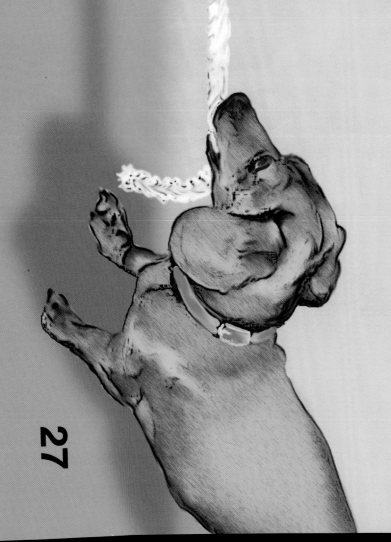

Now you have just one parent—
Soon it will be two."

The three of them shared a hug
And the pups both gave a smile,
Knowing very soon
Their love would multiply.

28